The Great
Mouse Detective

Random House  New York

Library of Congress Cataloging-in-Publication Data: Walt Disney Pictures presents The great mouse detective. (Disney's wonderful world of reading ; 55) SUMMARY: The evil Ratigan plans to kidnap the queen and replace her with a life-size toy queen through whom he will rule England; but master mouse detective Basil of Baker Street steps in to foil the plot. Based on the Disney movie of the same title. [1. Mystery and detective stories. 2. Mice—Fiction. 3. England—Fiction] I. Walt Disney Pictures. II. Title: Great mouse detective. III. Series. PZ7.G7998 1986 [E] 86-42608 ISBN: 0-394-88497-3 (trade); 0-394-98497-8 (lib. bdg.)

Manufactured in the United States of America   4   D E F G H

It was a quiet night in old London.
Dawson was reading his newspaper.
"There's going to be quite a birthday party for the queen tonight," he said to his friend Basil.

But Basil did not answer.

The great mouse detective was busy with an experiment.

Queen's Party Tonight

The doorbell rang
just then.
Ding! Dong!
Basil did not seem
to hear that, either.
So Dawson went
to the door himself.

A little girl
was standing there.
She looked
very upset.

"I am Olivia Flaversham," she said.
"And I must see Mr. Basil right away.
You see, my father has been kidnapped.
Mr. Basil must help me find him."

Dawson brought Olivia in to meet Basil.
"Really, Dawson," said Basil. "I just
do not have time to chat with children."

"A bat with a wooden leg kidnapped my father and— Look! There's the bat now!" Olivia said.

She pointed to the window.

"Bat! Wooden leg! Why didn't you say so before?" cried Basil.

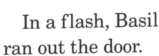

In a flash, Basil ran out the door.

"We must find that bat!" said Basil
as he and the others ran into an alley.
"His name is Fidget and he works
for the evil Ratigan."

"Look—tracks!" Basil said. "And they
were made by a wooden leg. It's Fidget!"

"I wonder whose cap this is," said Dawson. "I must show it to Basil."

"Good work, Dawson. This is Fidget's cap," said Basil.

"Now we must find Toby. He'll track down that wicked rat," Basil went on.

"Hello, old boy!" shouted Basil
when he saw Toby. "We are on a case
and we need your help. Here, smell
this cap."

Basil held up
the cap.
Toby's nose
began to twitch.

Then Toby started
to growl.
Basil picked up
Toby's leash.
There was no time
to lose!

Basil hooked the leash to Toby's collar.
Now Toby was ready for the hunt.

"Your father is as good as found,"
Basil told Olivia. "Come, Toby!"
Off went the dog and off went
the great mouse detective and
his friends!

Toby raced through the streets
of London.

At last he stopped in front
of a building and let off
his riders.

Basil and his friends
waved good-bye to Toby.
"I know where we are,"
said Olivia. "My father
works in this toy shop!"

"Aha! Here is
a secret door,"
said Basil.
 The door
swung open.
 Basil went
in first.

"We must be quiet,"
said Basil. "I'm sure
Fidget is in here
somewhere."

Fidget was in the toy shop.
Basil did not see him, but Fidget
saw Basil and Olivia and Dawson.

"More footprints!" said Basil.
"Fidget is close by.

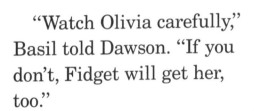

"Watch Olivia carefully,"
Basil told Dawson. "If you
don't, Fidget will get her,
too."

Dawson promised
to watch Olivia.
But he turned away
for just a moment.
And Olivia wandered
off to look at a toy.

Poor Olivia!
The moment Fidget saw she was alone,
he swooped down and threw her in a sack.
Then off he went with her.

Basil saw what
was happening.
He and Dawson
ran after Fidget.

But they were too late.
Fidget reached an open window
and disappeared.

"Dawson!" cried Basil.
"I told you not to leave
Olivia alone!"
Dawson said nothing.
It was all his fault.

"If only I
could find her,"
Dawson said
to himself.

Just then,
Dawson spotted
a slip of paper
on the floor.
What could
it be?
He showed
the paper
to Basil.

gears
crown
robe
little girl

Basil's face lit up.
"Dawson, you've done it!
This is a wonderful clue,"
he said. "I know where
Fidget has taken Olivia.
Ratigan has her. This list
is in his handwriting.
We must hurry, Dawson,
before it's too late."

Meanwhile, Ratigan was busy bragging
to his gang about his latest plot.
   "Today is the queen's birthday.
What a pity it will be her last!"
Ratigan said with a wicked grin.
"And guess who will be king then?
Me—Ratigan!"

Then Ratigan opened a door.
"I have a surprise for you,"
he said to Mr. Flaversham.

Olivia ran into her father's arms.
"You are safe!" Mr. Flaversham cried.
"Yes," said Ratigan, "and Olivia
will stay safe if you do what I say."

Fidget pulled Olivia away from her father.
He popped the little girl into a bottle.

Then Mr. Flaversham rolled in his new toy.
"Ah, here is our new queen," said Ratigan.

"Once the toy queen puts on this robe and crown, no one will be able to tell her from the real queen," Ratigan said.

"Now follow me, boys!" Ratigan shouted to his gang. "We are off to the palace. The queen's birthday party just won't be a party without us! Ha, ha, ha!"

Soon after Ratigan and his gang
had gone, Basil and Dawson reached
Ratigan's hideout.

"No one seems
to be here,"
said Basil.

Then they saw a big bottle.
"It's Olivia!" said Basil.

Basil tugged at
the cork until—
POP!—out it came.
"Mr. Basil!
Mr. Dawson!"
cried Olivia.
"I knew you
would find me."

"Ratigan has gone to the palace,"
Olivia told them as they ran outside.
"He had my father make a toy queen.
Ratigan is planning to get rid of
the real queen so he can be king!"

Basil knew what to do.
He whistled for Toby.

In an instant
Toby was there.

They climbed aboard the dog.
"To the palace!" said Basil.
"Be quick about it, old boy!"
And off they went.

Meanwhile, Ratigan was busy plotting.
"Nothing can stop me now!" he said
in a low voice. "Everybody here thinks
that is their beloved queen, but I have
the real queen locked away!"

The toy queen's voice sounded just
like the voice of the real queen.
"Good evening. Thank you for coming
to my party," said the toy queen.

"I have been your queen for many years,"
the toy queen went on. "But I am growing
old. It is time for a change. I want you
to meet your new king, Ratigan the First."

"I am your new king," said Ratigan. "I plan to stay king for years. Do you understand?

"Every day is a work day from now on. And all the money you make goes to me, King Ratigan.

"And if anyone doesn't like it, that is too bad. Because what I say is the law!"

But just then
a door burst open.

"Don't listen to him!"
Basil shouted to the crowd.

"Ratigan has kidnapped the real queen.
That queen next to him is just a toy!"
Basil shouted.

"Curses—it's Basil!" Ratigan snarled.
"I'm getting out of here fast!"

Ratigan turned and ran.
The toy queen fell over.
"Guards, stop that man!"
Basil cried as he and Dawson
chased after Ratigan.

The guards grabbed Ratigan and Fidget.
The rule of King Ratigan was over!
The real queen would be set free.
Olivia and her father were back together.
"Mr. Basil! Mr. Dawson!" said Olivia.
"I knew you would help me. Thank you!"
Basil told a reporter what had happened.

The next evening, Dawson sat
in Basil's living room, reading
the newspaper.

"Well, Basil, you really saved
the day," Dawson said.

But Basil did not answer.

He was working on a new case.

It was all in a day's work
for the great mouse detective!

Ratigan Arrested

Queen Honors Detective